Roger Duvoisin

Periwinkle

Alfred A. Knopf New York

This is a Borzoi book published by Alfred A. Knopf, Inc. Copyright © 1976 by Roger Duvoisin. All rights reserved under International and Pan-American Copyright Conventions. Published in the United States by Alfred A. Knopf, Inc., New York, and simultaneously in Canada by Random House of Canada Limited, Toronto. Distributed by Random House, Inc., New York. *Library of Congress Cataloging in Publication Data.* Duvoisin, Roger Antoine, 1904–   Periwinkle. SUMMARY: A lonely giraffe and frog must overcome their tendency to talk without listening before they can become friends. [1. Animals—Fiction.   2. Friendship—Fiction]   I. Title   PZ7.D957Pd3   [E]   76-8665   ISBN 0-394-83298-1   ISBN 0-394-93298-6 lib. bdg. Manufactured in the United States of America

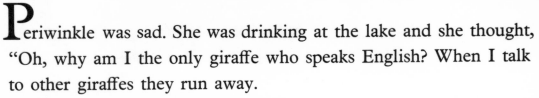

Periwinkle was sad. She was drinking at the lake and she thought, "Oh, why am I the only giraffe who speaks English? When I talk to other giraffes they run away.

"When I talk to antelopes they bleat.

Zebras whinny.

Hippopotamuses groan.

Rhinoceroces grunt.

Elephants trumpet.

Buffaloes bellow.

No one to talk to. I am so lonely."

"I speak English," a little voice said suddenly out of somewhere. Periwinkle jumped joyfully. Where did the voice come from?

"I am here in the water," said the voice. "I am Lotus the frog. How wonderful to meet someone I can talk to. I am so lonely."

"So am I," said Periwinkle. "But how can a frog speak English?"

"I learned it when I lived in an aquarium. But how can a giraffe speak English?"

"I learned it when I lived in a zoo. Periwinkle is my name. I am happy to talk to you. I have so much to say."

"So have I. But you are so tall, Periwinkle. It hurts my neck to look up at you."

"And it hurts mine to bend down to you, Lotus. Why not sit on my head? Then we could talk more easily." Periwinkle bent her head all the way down to Lotus.

"Good idea," said Lotus, and she jumped onto Periwinkle's head.

They were each so pleased to have found someone to talk to that they both began talking at the same time.

"I am proud to be a giraffe but
   "For an educated frog like me
at times I find it tiresome for
   life is dull among frogs
with a long long neck and long legs
   who croak day and night.
I cannot possibly sit to rest.
   In good English I say, stop—
STOP? STOP! You'd better STOP and let ME speak!
   BUT IT'S YOU WHO TALK AND TALK AND TALK!

WILL YOU LISTEN NOW!

SHOW SOME MANNERS PLEASE!

CUT OUT THAT PRATTLE!

STOP YOUR NOISE!

SILLY CROAKER!"

EMPTY WINDPIPE!"

"GO JUMP IN THE LAKE!" shouted Periwinkle.

"GLADLY!" cried Lotus, and she bit Periwinkle's ear as she jumped.

"Ouch, ouch!" screamed Periwinkle, and she lunged forward to catch Lotus. But Periwinkle slipped into the deep lake and had to lift her head high to keep from drowning. "Help, help, help!" she cried.

"Ha, ha," said Lotus, swimming around Periwinkle's head. "Now you will have to listen to *me* instead of talking and talking."

Poor Periwinkle could neither talk nor listen, for her mouth
and ears were full of water. However, she quickly waded out of the
lake when she saw a crocodile swimming toward her.

Sad and lonely, Periwinkle went back to the silent trees.

"No one to talk to," she wailed.

"No one to listen to me.

"NO ONE TO LISTEN TO ME! Now that I think of it, Lotus might have listened to me if I had listened to her. I must see her again."

Off she galloped to the lake to talk to Lotus.

"That's what I was thinking too," said Lotus. "And I am sorry I was mean to you."

"Then jump on my head again," said Periwinkle, bending her neck down. "I am so impatient to hear all you have to say."

So Lotus jumped and sat on Periwinkle's head.

"Please," she said, "tell me your stories first."

"No, I would like to hear your own stories first."

"Oh, I wouldn't be so rude as to talk before listening to you."

"That's also how I feel. Please talk first."

"Please, after you."

"No, no, after you."

"No, no, no, please."

"NO NO NO NO NO!"

"No?" said Lotus. "Then *I* will tell you this. I am wasting my time. First you only talk and talk and now you only want to listen."

"And since that's what you are doing yourself, I no longer want you on top of my head," answered Periwinkle.

She shook her head with such anger that Lotus fell to the ground, where she lay quite still.

Before Lotus could crawl back to the lake, a hungry jackal picked her up and ran off to eat her.

But then Periwinkle chased the jackal along the shore of the lake with all the speed in her long legs.

She caught him by his tail and pulled so hard he dropped Lotus, who rolled into the water. She was safe.

While Lotus rested among the croaking frogs and the silent fish, Periwinkle, more and more lonely and gloomy, went back to the silent trees.

"No one to talk to," she wailed and moaned.

"No one to listen to me. No one to talk *with*.

"Ha . . . NO ONE TO TALK *WITH*! That's it. No wonder Lotus and I could not be friends. We must talk *with each other* instead of only talking or listening! I'll see how she feels."

So Periwinkle galloped back to the lake.

"Oh," said Lotus, "I am only a little bruised, but I think we were *both* stupid."

"Jump back then and sit on my head. We will never be lonely again."

And Lotus made herself comfortable on Periwinkle's crown.

"Tell me, Lotus, is it nice to live in an aquarium?"

"Bad and good. I had a tiny tank of water to bathe in and a tiny spot for sleeping. No room to swim or go exploring. So boring. How was it in your zoo?"

"Bad and good, too. A room under a roof and a small yard outside to see the sun. No place to walk or run. But what was good in your aquarium?"

"There were good things to eat. And it was fun to watch through the glass wall and see the queer people who walked by. Their young ones talked and sang a lot to me. That's how I learned English."

"It was the same in my zoo. Good things to eat and fun to watch the people behind the bars. There were fat and thin ones, hairy and bald ones, tall and short ones, old and young ones. What crazy creatures there are in this world! The young ones threw peanuts at me. They talked and sang to me. That's how I learned English."

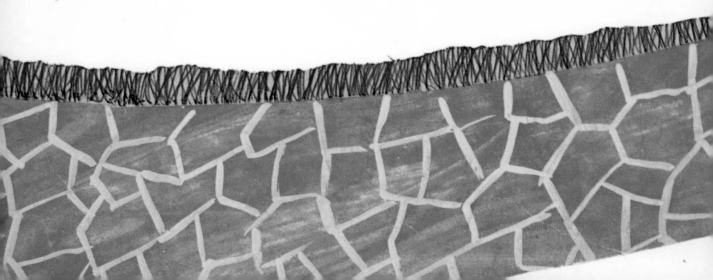

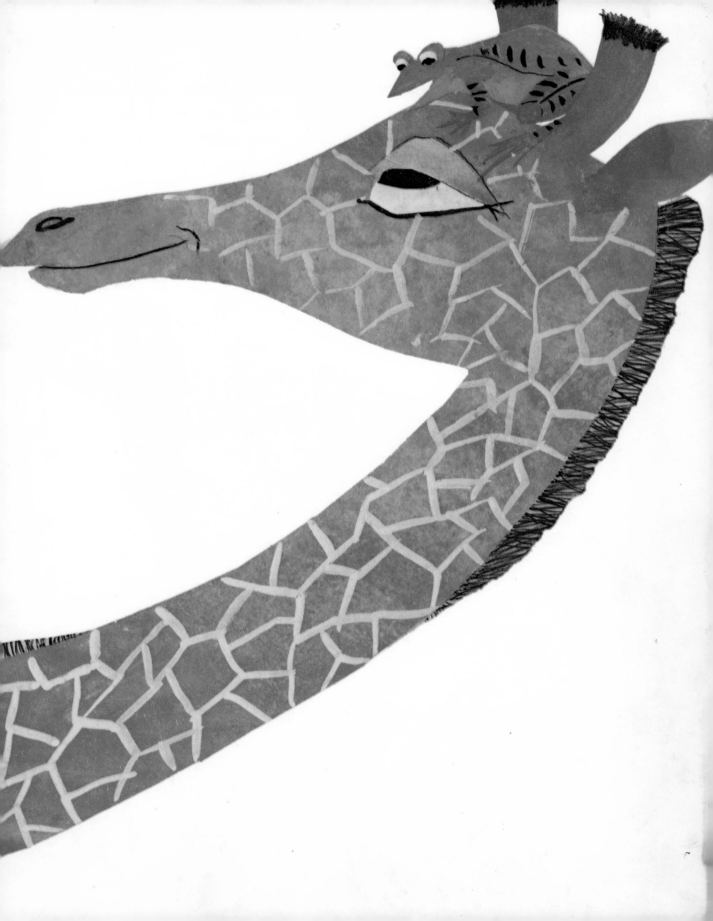

And so, Periwinkle and Lotus went on talking. Lotus wove a fine grass nest for herself between Periwinkle's horns, and every day thereafter they talked *with* each other, and they became good friends.

Birds flew around them to sing and share in their happiness. They were never lonely again.